Tying The Threads

Louise Barrette

Legal Disclaimer

TYING THE THREADS

~ Content Advisory~

The contents disclosed in this literature are for educational purposes only. The content in this book contains strong subject matter. My hope with this book is to raise awareness to victims who have had to endure evil. This book is based on true events. Names, dates and places have been changed to protect the rights of individuals mentioned.

~ DEDICATIONS~

Dedicated to my son Michel and anyone who has ever faced injustices during their life journey.

~ TABLE OF CONTENTS~

PART TWO

~ TABLE OF CONTENTS~

~Chapter One~

The Adoption

In a little village called Hawkesbury, located in Canada. A baby was born, it was a beautiful sunny day, on the fifteenth of July 1967. The baby had bright blue eyes, a tiny, beautiful face and blonde hair. Despite the beauty of this baby, she was born and given up for adoption.

The cries had already begun, burying me starting from birth, for an unknown world was awaiting, indeed for me. Sitting on the floor in this strange place of life, it really had begun in my mind. This place was full of cries, and babies all over. This place called Children's Aid, was a nightmare for the workers. I had this nice woman called Mrs. D. Jones, who was assigned to my case file and she was going to find me a home. All of this so I could have a family and joy. Today, a lot wiser old, I can still remember how it all happened.

TYING THE THREADS

The reoccurring dreams wavering in and out of my mind for many years. I would say my life has always been with many struggles. Even today I feel much sadness, waiting for someone to truly love me. My life has been filled with tragedy and pain. The contents disclosed in my book, wont be easy or full of happiness, but rather a testament of my strength.

I remember sitting semiquaver on the floor of the Children's Aid's Office. We were awaiting for my sempiternal family. I can still remember as if it was yesterday. I remember the fear, anxiety, and cries of that building. I often had dreams about this lady picking me up in her arms and giving me away. Those dreams lead me to find this lady from Children's Aid, after twenty- five years of not seeing her.

I had went to the office of Children's Aid, looked around and then pointed her out. I walked towards her and said; *"Hello, Mrs. Jones, you're probably wondering who I am right?"* She said; *"YES, who are you?"* gazing back at me, she looked puzzled. Then I answered; *"You were the one that picked me up and gave me away as a child."* I had been able to find her because of all the dreams I had often experienced. I could still remember her face and the gloominess that haunted her eyes.

I had reminded Mrs. Jones of my name and she said: "*Oh God! You are right, it is you, do you ever have a good memory, this can't be.*" She couldn't believe it and was very shocked that I had remembered her, from my dreams. Mrs. Jones kept saying "*IN YOUR DREAMS?*" I started telling her a bit about my dreams, and how it all went. I could see her picking me up from a corner in an old house. A house which was right in the middle of the Village in Alfred, Ontario.

There was an old brown rug and I was sitting, pondering on. Mrs. Jones, she was in a coequal state of shock, and very surprised. She was so stunned that her mind was wayfaring. We then sat quietly for a while. Then she asked me how I had been doing since the adoption. I had lucked out, because I was adopted by two loving parents that had hearts of gold. The couple were childless, which was why they had chosen to adopt two little girls. They adored us very much; one was named Louise and the other —Jocelyne. Of course I am Louise, and that meant I had also gained a sister.

This establishment called Children's Aid, was a nightmare. It reminded me of a grocery store, with a price tag on each one of us. We would only be hearing the ticking of the anticipation that had filled our minds.

I asked Mrs. Jones why; she allowed them to daze with dearness at us. Both parents admiring us with their eyes full of glitter and happiness. We were about to embrace a new life, and a new beginning. I could not help but wonder, what the future held for us both.

~ Chapter Two~
Nostalgia, Candy, & Tears

W e lived on a farm where we had cows, bulls, horses and a lot of mice. Of course there weren't supposed to be there —those little mice. Our parents gave us all the love they could, and a roof over our heads. They brought us to church, every Sunday. Between me and Jocelyne, I was what they call the little devil and my sister was the angel. Not an inch of my hair stayed in place, hers was always still.

Being the little rascal and up at six o'clock, I was outside as soon as the sun came up. It was ravishing. First thing I did when I got up was to— follow my dad around. Sometimes I would also just go play in the corn fields. I would be running around and often watch the sun get brighter. Then I would consider that my parents might be looking for me. I would go running back home, hoping not to have worried them all that much. As always, only my father would be looking for me, because that's how it worked in our home.

TYING THE THREADS

I was my father's favorite and my sister would be my mom's favorite. Jocelyne would only wake up at around eleven o'clock in the morning and she never gave any trouble. Jocelyne was always calm but sometimes lazy.

The love would always be there equally for us both though. I had found that we just connected with our parents in a unique way individually. My sister and I differed in personality, but it made our family our own. At the age of five years old, it was time for us to start school. My sister and I went to Ecole St-Victor in Alfred, Ontario. We also had started ballet lessons and piano. Weekdays we focused on school and our lives were always very full. Saturdays was our piano lessons, that took place during the afternoon. Besides being very busy, we still found time to go play with our friends.

We took our courses given by a brother of the Church, known as the Alfred reform Jail. This brother when giving us the classes, would make us sit down in a perfect position. He would make us sit, with our hands always on top. This was to make sure we didn't touch the border of the piano. If we did, he would hit our hands with a ruler. It hurt us a lot and we were often afraid.

TYING THE THREADS

I did make it to six University Degrees in Piano. To this day, I still have bad dreams regarding the hitting of my hands. My childhood was filled with unique experiences, that shaped who I am today. A fond memory of my childhood was that my parents had bought us a pool, which I thought was so very nice.

We also owned a little shanty where we would go play with our dolls. We were always fed very well, and if you were looking for me, I was always to be found in the garden. Found in gardens where green was the colors of the lands. Lands where my daily memories of my childhood —still play in my mind.

In our first year at school, we were very eager to start of course. When you start school, everyone gets assigned to a tutor. Mine was so very kind and her name was Nadia. Sometimes we would be playful and it would be pleasant. One time Nadia came to get me and I didn't want to go with her for my lesson. So, I took her hand and bite her. In those days, so young I just wanted to play freely. Of course, I never meant to hurt her and I was just a child, but I do recall this moment. We saw each other later on in life, and I apologized. We both laughed at this incident, because well although it was really funny —-she still carried the bite mark on her hand. I was such a wild and restless child. My mother of course knew it.

TYING THE THREADS

Oftentimes I would observe my family and leave to go rollerblading, with my friends. Often I would hear my dad calling for me. I also spent my time with some of my extended family, one being—my mom's sister. My aunt was a nun and would come over on the weekends. I loved her so much.

These relationships profoundly impacted me growing up. The things she would always bring for me and the things we did together, often made me happy. I remember one night I couldn't sleep and I went to sleep with her. I had a dream I was peeing in the toilet that night. We had woke up because I had peed on her and in the bed. she screamed, but we ended up laughing about it and she forgave me.

All of these profound memories have impacted me in some way. I recall reaching grade three in school. My teacher, Mrs. Day was a very nice teacher. At one time she gave us a test and told us that whoever wrote from 1 to 100 the fastest would win a plane toy. There was twenty-two of us in the classroom. Of all the odds, me and another boy won. We had finished first at the same time so we each got a little plane toy. Just those little things when you're in little school that make you so happy.

TYING THE THREADS

On another day, in the winter months our whole classroom was wondering and looking outside at the fence. I was dared to go put my tongue on it to see if it was true that it would stick there. Of course, as naive as I was, I did it. My tongue was stuck on that fence for hours, leaving me feeling embarrassed. Everyone was laughing at me, until a teacher came out and had poured water on my tongue and it unglued to the fence. I was bleeding, crying, and humiliated. I choose to accept the challenge and decided that I needed to be brave.

This little school, it was supposed to be pleasant, but it's funny how back in the older days things were so different. I was always at the principal's office, at least once a week with the same others getting the 1-foot hard strap. The strap was given either on our hands or on our bottoms. After being asked where we wanted it, from this principal. Times have certainly changed and its hard to believe at one point, this was considered normal. My parents often got tired of hearing me cry every day, and so they had started researching schools for me. I was entering grade six at the time of these changes. My mom found a private girl's school in Vankleek Hills. Nuns were the owners, and the teachers of this place called a Convent.

TYING THE THREADS

You would get there on Sunday nights, then you would be picked up on Fridays at noon. Sunday nights you could hear all the girls crying just for having been brought to the convent home. Some were sick already and didn't want to be there.

This place was huge, held over 100 dormitories, a chapel, around twenty classrooms, and two large dining rooms. Each dining room held around one hundred students and also had three big playrooms. The convent had many, many stairs, and all the teachers were Nuns. In each of these little rooms we had a washing bowl, a bed, and a small closet.

So, grade six had passed, then grade seven and then grade eight had started. This convent was sometimes a fun place to be, but also a place at other times we just wanted to run away. When we were eating, some girls decided to play jokes of initiation. The girls would put salt, in the sugar box. Since I loved sugar, I had poured salt in my cereal, and the nuns would force us to eat it or we would be punished. Even sometimes when they would cook eggs, they would not cook them well. The eggs were so gooey and slimy, and I had put a lot on my plate and what a mistake that was.

TYING THE THREADS

I was left for two- hours in the dining room, forced to eat these eggs that were sitting on my plate. It was hell. Overall, my childhood was made up of fond memories, some good and some unpleasant. It was proof that despite the circumstances we are born into, a sense of nostalgia is always prominent as humans.

My dear fun had come to an end in May of 1981 when my mom had called the convent, to let the nuns know what had happened. My mom had told the Nuns that she was going to pick up Jocelyne and I. My parents had told the Nuns not to tell us anything. For me I thought she was just picking us up early because she had missed us.

When I got in the car it was my cousin Robert who was driving. My mom had tears in her eyes. I got scared and asked her what was wrong and then she turned around and said that my that my father had passed away. My Father passed away because he had suffered his fourth hearth attack. This was devastating to me, as my father was my everything. My father worked a lot and worked hard to provide for his family. He had worked all his life, at the Ottawa General Hospital as a Porter.

TYING THE THREADS

My father had a big garden, a farm at home, a water delivery company, acres of land with animals, a cheese factory, and lastly— fifteen acres of corn fields. I remember my father with his water truck company. My father was on a delivery to another man's farm, where there was a lot of horses. This farm had around 135 horses.

When the older man saw me, he turned and noticed that I was admiring a specific horse. He then asked me if I wanted the horse because he was seeing a connection from me and this specific horse and told me to ask my father. I said, *"hold on yes, I will ask my father."* I then proceeded to ask my father and he had said yes. I was so happy and could not believe, that I was bringing this horse home.

The older man said; *"Don't worry! I will bring it to your house by daylight the following day."* He asked me what I would name him, I said *"Candy."* I couldn't wait till the next day to wake up and see if it was real. Of course, the next morning I was up by 6am and the first thing I did was look outside and there was Candy—my horse.

TYING THE THREADS

The things I remember about Candy, were that I was only one that could approach him. He did not like anyone else but me. At one point my father had tried to approach Candy and the horse would lift up, to scare my father away. I was the only one who could interact with Candy without signs of trouble.

If you remember I had told you that in the Village of Alfred, Ontario, we had a place called College of Reform for men. It was a jail and sometimes these guys would run away. One time one man had run away and was found in our barn where Candy was. This barn is where my father also had his fourth heart attack and I was the one who had found my dad, along with everything else. Life would change starting now, and forever.

However, coming back to us being picked up at the convent and being told my father had died of his fourth heart attack. My memories would change from happier ones to unpleasant ones. Before arriving to our house, I saw many cars and I was extremely scared. My mother started to cry because she knew I wasn't going to be okay with all this news. I got out of the car and ran into the house. I avoided eye contact with everyone. I ran to my room and began to scream and cry.

I threw everything that I could find everywhere, breaking things and crying. My sister handled it a lot calmer than I could. I turned into this person that I no longer recognized. I didn't even know myself any longer or what was happening anymore. Just screaming *"This can't be happening."* I couldn't believe my father was gone. Days passed, and we had the funeral. Since my father was part of The Chevalier Colomb all the members were there, his friends, our family, our friends from school, and many more. When he was exposed, I went for a walk.

Since I was in grade eight, going into grade nine in Alfred. There was always an initiation where if you got caught, they would throw eggs at you, and much more. It just so happened that it was my turn for the egging and I had walked into it that night. I was assaulted and they didn't know I was at my father's funeral that day, but I was in trouble even still.

My mother eventually found me sitting in front of the store and started screaming at me that it wasn't time to be playing. I was crying devastated and trying to tell her what had happened. She told me to get in the car and was just as shocked as I was.

TYING THE THREADS

When we buried my father it was so important that the members of The Chevalier Colomb were all lined up and also dressed up. Dressed in armour suits and hats while lifting up the coffin. After the funeral— I knew our lives would change forever. It started with an auction, selling all his machinery for farming. Even his water truck, the cows, and my horse. I didn't know who I was anymore, who knew what they would do with me. Inside of my mind and heart, I would talk to my father and ask him to protect me in all this.

We had plans before his passing, we were supposed to buy this home, I remember it very well, down Smyth Road in Ottawa, right in front of the school. We were going to attend for grade nine, where suits were brown and beige. Another private school but boys were there this time, who would be attending. Well, we never did buy that house and other plans started to fade and some news ones had begun. One of my mother's sister's Agathe Chiasson, was suddenly living at our house in Alfred. Agatha began taking care of us and our mother, was glued to us, telling my mother to sell everything and fast.

TYING THE THREADS

My aunt made us leave our piano lessons, our ballet classes, guitar, flute, and majorettes. The worst was her coming to tell my mother to sell the family home, and our farm. She wanted us to move in with her in the City of Ottawa, to a small appartement.

For me I became so scared, my father had passed away and I had to see everything fall apart. A reality now tearing us apart. My mother was getting sick because she missed my father so very much, she couldn't bare having lost my father. I could also not bare the weight of grief and loss.

I remember I was coming down the stairs from my bedroom, I then saw my aunt. She had on only a bra and a slip skirt. She was asking or should I say telling my mom she had to sell everything asap and move to Ottawa. Right away. I screamed and took a drawer not realizing what was in it. I threw it at my aunt and began screaming *"we are not moving anywhere"* telling her to stop and this was too quick. Unfortunately, this drawer was the one holding all the best knifes we had, and she sustained just a few scratches.

TYING THE THREADS

Well, to my aunt it was just the situation that would give her an advantage and she turned and looked at me and said that *" I had done it"* that this was it and she called the police and Children's Aid. My mother never had any chance to talk to me. I was screaming and crying. I said; *"No not this, mom no, please don't let her do this."* Well, I was placed with Children's Aid and moved to Bourget, to another good family home.

~ Chapter 3 ~

Not One, But Both

My Life changed very quickly, now while living with this new family. I had overheard that my aunt had been thrown out of our family home. My mother reminded her that —I was also grieving. My mother said that she wasn't going anywhere and to stay, until she figures things out. Bourget was not too far from Alfred, and the family I was living with also had family in Alfred. They lived right on the highway in the village of Alfred.

They owned a French fry stand and in front of their house, there was a huge deck to sit on and look at traffic. They also had a daughter my age and while sitting and looking at cars passing, we then saw a car being towed. It was a bad accident telling from the shape of the car. The more it came closer, the more I could see —that it was my mother's car. I couldn't believe it was my mother's car. She was the one that had the accident, just one day before she was supposed to pick me up from this family. The family with whom I was living at in Bourget.

TYING THE THREADS

I ran inside telling this family and I was screaming, that I just seen my mother's car in the back of a tow truck. After the foster family heard my concerns, they allowed me to call home. My suspicions were true; it was my mother. My sister Jocelyne answered and said she was home with our cousins and that they were heading to the hospital. Before I even had time to ask to tell her where I was, so someone could pick me up—she hung up the telephone. No one ever picked me up. When my father had passed it was already unbearable and now my sister was beside my injured mother and I was left behind. My father had died May 1983 and on November 11, 1983— was my mom's car accident. My mother's passing was on the 11th of November 1984. One year exactly in the hospital she had spent, fighting for her life.

No one ever picked me up. I never got to be by my mother's bed side during her ailment's or passing. It left me feeling abandoned and left out. A week had passed with the new family where I had begun living. My new family were the ones that arranged for me to visit my mother, they are the ones that made the decision. They knew it wasn't right what was happening. While I was beside her the only thing, I was saying in my mind was *"Please don't take her too, please God this would be too hard."*

TYING THE THREADS

Later that same day, I called home again to try to find out what had happened to my mother and my sister. My aunt had told me that she had gone to Ottawa to buy herself a nice suit, because she had nothing nice enough to wear to come pick me up. She was picking me up from this family's home in Bourget. They started telling me that it was my fault that my mother had this accident. They claimed that it would have never happened if she never had to pick me up and I answered with; *"why did no one go with her?"* She hung up the phone and never talked to me again until Christmas.

Now of course I know nothing would be the same anymore and I knew I was never coming back home to my room or that I would never get to see my things again. I kept asking God why both my parents? Why take both? I had many questions. While still living in Bourget there was this girl that came to live there also and she would always try to run away and eventually she got placed in the city in a new home. When she left we both cried and said that we would write to each other and stay in touch. Two weeks later, I had a call that she wanted to see me. She was in the hospital with a third- degree burn, resulting from using products for floors. She had sustained injury while cleaning on her knees and putting some dangerous wax on these floors.

TYING THE THREADS

This happened while she had a cigarette ignited and she caught on fire. She had so many bandages and was crying when she saw me. We both were crying. I can still hear her saying my name as I entered the room. Today she is fine, living with the scars and living with her own family. At a very young age, I had seen and experienced a lot of loss, grief, and abandonment—since birth. I was young and struggled understanding the things that had happened to me, even to this day.

Starting at an innocent age admittedly, I didn't know the value of money. My parents had never shown that they had a lot of money. We had to go to church every Sunday for me to have my very first pair of jeans. They had worked all their lives, just to put money away. They only money part I remember as a child, is when the neighbor's house caught fire. My mother had given me a little cardboard box and told me to go sit by my barbie house and wait for her to call me to come in. I went in the little house and of course was told not to open that box. I opened it and it was well packed and full of one-hundred-dollar bills.

TYING THE THREADS

I thought to myself if I take one, she will never know and so I did, and not too long after I hear my mother calling me telling me it's safe to come back and bring back the box. Just one hour later she called me back in the house and asked me if I took something. I said *"Of course not."* She gazed at me and told me *"Louise, I know you took one- hundred-dollars from it all."*

I was shocked and gave it back. You see how calculated she was. So, it's obvious the family knew how much money they had. While my mother was in the hospital, every family member would come sit beside my mom trying to get her to sign the will. They had prepared the paperwork in their names and in which they had to write it in to take care of us till we were 18-years old.

My mother had a few sisters. There was, Cecile, Agathe, Beatrice, and Rosalia. There was also two brothers — Andre and Phillippe. The part where that hurts me the most, is the wills they would bring, but that they never wanted to see me. I could see what they were doing. The only thing in their heads was the thought of the money and who was going to win.

TYING THE THREADS

I still think of my aunt Agatha and how she would sit at the end of my mom's bed. She would stick needles in my mom's toe, trying to wake her up. This was so my mother would sign the will over to her. Nurses would see this too, but when they seen on the spot they would ask them to leave. My mother had a head tumor, making her deteriorate. So, for them it was the fact of not knowing who was going to win and gain access to her funds. For me, it was who would take care of me and my sister.

We temporarily lived with my cousin named Robert, in his home in Ottawa. Of which again my sister was already there. I was picked up on the 25th of December 1983, which was the exact day. So, my mother in the end signed the will to my cousin Robert.

~ Chapter 4~

For The Love of Money

When my parents were alive, they did house her brother Andre's children. They were from New Brunswick but stayed at our house in Alfred. This was so they could go to the Ottawa University for a few years. My parents did this at no cost, because my parents loved them as their own also. They were also from my dad's side of the family. My father had twin brother's, who had two daughters —that also lived with us.

Our home was massive and housed many extended family members. A home that was full of love. Every year at Christmas, it was celebrated at our house and our family was fairly large. The same as every other holiday. Since my parents had passed away, I never saw any holiday celebrations or asked to go anywhere. I lost my whole family, because of money.

TYING THE THREADS

We were young, innocent, and didn't understand what money had to do with any of it. We never knew how much money our parents had. We just knew, the situation and circumstances were awful and would highly affect us. My whole family seemed to know how much money my parents had acquired throughout their lives. Which is probably why they always visited and sucked up. They would try and be nice with us. The worst was that my cousin kept us away from anyone who would come near us. My cousin would say that he won custody of us, and he was very smart and we would see. He did what was written in the will but re-arranged it— as things went along. One thing that was not said in the will, was to threaten a 14-year-old girl. I was threatened and told if I did not sign ten out of my fifteen bonds, there would be trouble. They were worth thousands of dollars each.

My cousin said if I didn't sign, I wouldn't have clothes to go to school, or any food. Of course I signed, but I was also very scared. I knew it was wrong, but what if it was true. I did go with him to the bank to sign them over. Looking at tellers with a story in my eyes, for which I was hoping they would make it stop.

TYING THE THREADS

The worst is looking back at this will today, I also paid for my own Christmas gifts given from my cousin. Even my calls I made to the hospital, my rent to him and to another place I was living. The sickening amount was one million-two-hundred and fifty dollars. Two houses along with three pieces of land property. My cousin Robert lived in Vanier, Ontario right near my new dedicated high school. It was only two steps away from my front door. That was the rest of January 1984.

When my mother was still in the hospital Robert was also not married and two other men were living there. I did not feel this was good judgement call. Having be that that we lived there, in a home full of men. When we were misbehaving, he would send us to our room. It was mostly me of course, because my sister has always been no trouble and considered the angel. I was always in my bedroom and he would lock me in there with the help of locks. This was often difficult for me, being isolated and kept inside my room a lot.

I just wanted to be beside my mothers' bed at the hospital because at the time she was dying of cancer, and a brain tumor. So, one night I made the decision to think of a way that I could run away and pondered all the possibilities.

TYING THE THREADS

I jumped out of the window and put one foot out and had one foot inside. My options were if I fall inside, I stay, but if I fall outside, I run. There was a 9-foot fence with sharp ends that I had to jump over. I ended up falling out and I ran like hell. I punctured one hand very deeply; it was bleeding badly but still I ran. I took an OC transport bus. I explained to the bus driver what happened and when I got to the hospital, I explained everything to the nurse. She got me a little bed so I could sleep beside my mother's bed. The next day came the worst came; I couldn't even get anyone to let me explain a little bit about my cousin Robert's life. Every weekend while living at my cousin's house he would have a party where he would cook crab for him and his friends. Making us to stay in our bedrooms.

When we had first moved in he had a girlfriend name Debbie. Debbie was so beautiful, she had long blonde hair. I can still see her face in my mind. Once time I heard them fighting, they were talking so loudly, I came out of my room to make it stop. I recalled one time, he was hitting her and slapping her. It ended up that she left him — I never forgave him. My cousin had these eyes looking at me and turned back as I was going into my room. I was crying and thinking about how when someone is nice, they are often pushed too far. Another loss and more pain, id have to endure at a young age.

TYING THE THREADS

Forever imprinting my mind and distorting the way I saw my cousin. Now continuing back to my next awful day at the Hospital, I saw the police and Children's Aid walking towards my mother's room, along with my cousin. They sat me in front of my cousin and asked me what was wrong. I was so afraid of him that I said nothing. The police brought me right back home and more was added to my file at Children's Aid. I went to my room crying and tried to think of ways out and to never be found this time. For me I was just trying to find help. Again, I was left feeling like the problem, I was simply just trying to find my way in a crippling world of grief.

One week later I ended up walking 8-miles in the snow, since it was winter. I was given only running shoes and a light jacket. The reason was so that I couldn't run away again, because I'd freeze. It didn't matter to me if I froze because I needed help and I walked in the cold anyway. What happened you may wonder? Well now Children's Aid did not listen to me, instead drove me back to my cousins house. Not believing what my cousin did was wrong. Growing up I never had thoughts of running away, I was happy never did I need to run away. I used to run in corn fields and go to work with my father. We had animals on the farm, and we were living the life.

TYING THE THREADS

It was never shown that there was money involved. I feel like my forehead should have said in big writing; *"Enough, PLEASE HELP ME."* My sister she had already met her now husband, at the age of 15-years old. She is still with him, till this day. My sister moved out quickly from my cousin's house. Her life was already happily planned. My sister met her husband through a man from my father's work, named Pierre. He was always at our house helping my father. This one day he brought his little brother, which ended up being my sister's first crush and now— only husband.

Me and my father would sometimes play in the garden and pretend we both were falling in the garden from laughing so much, laughing to tears. Pierre was my fathers' best friend. Now some of my most memorable memories. Up until the age of seventeen, I have shared some of them.

~Chapter 5~

The Escape, Pregnancy, & Motorcycles

S ince I was terribly miserable and it felt like a jail at Robert's house, I gave a lot of thought and decided to run away for good. Making sure that no one would find me. Including the police or Children's Aid. I went to live with a girlfriend of mine, who wanted to help me. I stayed with her for a week. I met a guy named Gillus and made him my first. We had passionate intercourse. I kind of ran away from him because he was so possessive, just as much as my cousin was. It became too painful to relive this type of connection again.

I had gone back to my friend Johanne's house, but they had a big family and I felt like it was too much. The worst part was that I was almost found at her house. Then she talked about a friend, that didn't live too far from her house. I met this person and they seemed okay.

TYING THE THREADS

After being there for one-day, I found that there was a lot of in and out in that house. I would always wonder why but I didn't ask any questions. I took a bunk bed upstairs and I felt safe with these people that lived there. Which ended up one of my biggest mistakes ever to not have seen what was about to happen to me. Eventually I found out, this house was known for selling substances and the people that would come in and out were unknowns at times. Some ended up being so addicted to drugs, which ended up profoundly impacting my reality.

One night, one came into my room, while I was sleeping. I woke up and this man was sexually assaulting me. I remember I was screaming, but the music was too loud —no one heard me. I cried and cried. I never told anyone what had happened. I then called another girlfriend of mine to go live with her and her parents.

This incident changed me in a lot of ways and profoundly traumatized me. I would endure this awful incident, with many replays of memories until my life would turned around. I started to work at a movie theatre and I met my very first long-term boyfriend Michael. Me and Michael were so happy, so passionately in love. We were great together in the beginning.

TYING THE THREADS

I soon moved into his family home in Gatineau, Quebec. It was him and then his mother upstairs. We had the whole basement to ourselves. The passion sexually was perfect in every way. We had tried it all and explored one another on many levels. After being together for two years, my last month working at the movie theatre, Michael wanted to buy himself a Harley Davidson and I was fine with this, since one of his sister's, Micheline was married with a known biker club, they had a lot of great connections. Connections for the perfect motorcycle, at a low cost.

We went for a week, down to their home in St-Foy Quebec for a week. It was a beautiful drive. As we arrived there, it was welcoming. Arriving to their house was memorable, the home had stunning furniture. They owned a Pitbull, who had this huge metal necklace full of spikes. Admittedly I was scared. When Richard was around the dog was fine.

However, Richard would always go into the basement to work. I fell asleep on the couch and when I woke up, he dog was on top of me. This dog was growling like he wanted to eat me alive. I was whispering Richard's name, because I thought this was it for me. I held on to this necklace and a minute had passed. Richard just happened to come back up just in time and seen the dog.

TYING THE THREADS

Richard had shown us what the dog could do, as he was trained to hold on to a 5-foot bar with his teeth. The dog could tear a tire. This dog was very strong and obviously this incident made me feel uncomfortable. I looked at Michael later on and asked if we could leave earlier to make up an excuse. We came home 3-days earlier and I went back to work. Michael started to make friends who were bikers in our area in Gatineau, Quebec. One for sure was a younger kid, who Michael really got along well with. I thought he was so cute and Michael knew that. Michael had arranged for the kid's sister to hop on Michael's bike and for me to see her behind. When they showed up like this at my work, I panicked and thought he was hurting me right in my face and I started to run for the girl.

The kid got mad and started to try to ram me over with his Motorcycle. The story eventually came out and I apologized but they shouldn't have played a game like this without advising me first. And since Michael had bought his motorcycle, these games kept on coming unannounced. Since we lived together, we tried to make the best out of things in our lives.

We ended up going to visit his sister in Quebec, St-Joy for another weekend.

TYING THE THREADS

Richard, the sculpturer brought me to the basement to show me his work and oh my god, the basement was full of beautiful work he was doing. There was a huge bed with skeleton heads filled with real diamonds, and so much more. I had never seen such amazing wood working.

In the week we were there he gave me a sculpture kit and asked me to draw what I was the best at drawing. I drew a Harley Davidson since it was the only thing, I knew how to draw really well. He told me to bring it home and to sculp it. I told Richard I will and I will make you proud. It took me a full summer outside in the yard and I wouldn't stop until I was done. It is a great passion for me to be able to do this. When we went back up to St Foy Quebec, I showed Richard and he was going to train me some more to do big pieces, but he was amazed at the work I had already done.

I then told him someone is willing to pay me one-thousand dollars for my work. He told me "Sell it" and I did. Richard was such a good man and such a good brother-in-law. I had always thought of Bikers to be very bad people, but after getting to know some— most had great careers. For me Richard and Micheline were like gold, because they had shown me skills. Skills I had acquired forever and so I had thought, maybe one day I could take the business over. My biker story will come soon in this story, towards the end.

TYING THE THREADS

In the meantime, my sister Jocelyne's wedding was coming up and I known about it. My sister was so afraid of being close to me. Mind you, I did experiment with drugs but was never on them or was never an alcoholic either. I admit I was scary back then, not really me but the people that I hung around with. I had the HA on one side and the Mafia at some point. I was never invited to my sister's wedding and it hurt. I wanted to be there. I decided to show up with Michael anyway. My sister while walking back down the isle, saw me and started to cry and held me as we both cried. This was a memorable moment for me. The night would continue on, and it was a reminder of how in love with Michael I was and how passionate it was. Our love was supposed to be forever. It was amazing, but not far from another disaster.

Michael had started to go out alone with these guys to bars. My boyfriend was having too much fun —while leaving me home alone. Strip bars is where is he was also attending; I later found out. My mind started to become overwhelmed and of course I was very upset.

Until one night, he would come home and I began screaming and saying; *"You want to head out there now? Well, if you keep it up you will see me there one day soon."* He laughed and said; *sure.* Oh, but I meant it. I started to head out to meet all the guys downstairs. All the girls upstairs with my plan and practicing discussions. They were training me; I was training to be an exotic dancer while Michael was at work. I was sure he would show up while I was there.

I was so shy and I kept on telling all my new friends I will let you know when I am ready. So, I began planning to get him to see I was serious. Once I said I was ready, I had bought this bunny suit and some sexy lingerie and practiced. Some men were pigs and some were just there to talk and look. I made sure that my first- time on stage Michael was going to be there with his friends. Michael walked in with his friends and saw me and all hell broke loose. He ran toward me, grabbed me, and brought me outside to leave.

Michael was so upset that when he got on his motorcycle, he flipped it backwards. We discussed it and he promised he would stop going to those places, and it worked for a while and we were back to being happy. Michael and I were to be soon married and the games we played to each other caused a lot of pain. First loves are always painful because both are often young and still adventuring life.

We had hurt each other, using other people. But we managed to get through all of it— as our love was powerful. Then just when you think the problems are over… I followed Michael one night. I found him; to find him talking to this girl he had an affair with. I overheard her saying she was pregnant and so I ran home. I began waiting for the right time to confront him with this. Of course, Michael never shared this with me and time had passed, where I carried this inside of me for a long time.

Myself in the meantime I started to play games too and although I knew this guy was not for me I still saw this other guy to hurt Michael. As much as it hurt, I realized that we both didn't know any better. I did it to hurt Michael, as I was hurt from hearing the bad news. The news of this other girl , who was pregnant.

Our relationship was bound for war, the guy I was seeing behind Michaels back, knew I was about to inherit money and the whole time this guy was recently separated and had a daughter. Which he kept on telling me that I will marry him instead and this was it and with the money. He told me that we could get custody of his daughter because of the money coming my way. I got afraid and said; *" why is this my responsibility? "* Because I had said this, I soon had five people showing up at my door —which included him. I was so afraid that I had put scissors in my back of my pants just in case. That night, it turns out he beat up badly.

This guy is the one that brought me to the hospital while the doctor was asking me if I was able to tell him who did this to me. Meanwhile I gave this look to this guy. I looked at him with revenge in my eyes and thinking *" I will get you back."* Just so happened when I came out of the hospital, I was surrounded by these friends of Michaels and some of mine. I told this guy if you ever come close to me again " *I will tell and we'll see what would happen. "*

~ **Chapter Six** ~

Wedding Bells

My life was starting to haunt me with the different people from Michael's lifestyle. Michael had biker friends and Mafia friends from Toronto. I always remained clear of trouble so I could keep my good name. Even though I was surrounded by this lifestyle. I had some friends that all had Harley Davidsons and looked at me and said *"Well Louise were going back home we won't see you again, because we don't want to be blamed that we helped you spend money. "*So now me and Michael decided to have less friends for a while.

I received an inheritance and we moved to the home I had inherited, plus I was given my first amount of money. The wedding was to happen in two- months from the day we moved there. I ended up finishing my grade 12 a few months prior and time was approaching for this wedding. I had left my friends behind and he had left a lot of his guy friends. We were working normal jobs finally. Again, more chaos would erupt.

TYING THE THREADS

One-night Michael felt the need to go out and had asked me if it was okay if he went out with his friends. I had said of course and to go have fun. I ended up going in Hull, Quebec and stopped at the Rafman a very friendly bar. Upon entering this bar, my eye is quick to see Michael sitting with this girl in the bar. There she was the other women, I wondered why she was pregnant and in the bar with my soon to be husband. I confronted her and told her to go home and I would get an explanation later. It took a lot to calm me down that night. I did go home, with an array of emotions and anger.

When Michael came home he told me that she was not getting an abortion. She was going to keep the baby and it would change our relationship entirely. In fact, it would be the final chapter of it entirely. This was not something I could handle or accept. I got so upset that I called the wedding off and moved out a week later. I had went to live with a friend in Gatineau. His name was John but he was only a friend. I started to hang out in strip bars, but not partaking in dancing. I didn't need to...I was already given the beginning of my inheritance. I kept it quiet. John had a 3-Wheeler Harley Davidson.

TYING THE THREADS

My other Harley Davidson friends included a lot from ex groups— but we were all unnamed or from past groups. Some owned a Harley shop in Gatineau. Turns out this one night at the bar there was a tall handsome man who was there. The man was heaven to my eyes. I went to sit with him and started the conversation. Turns out these two were from the United States and were here on a business trip. They were FBI Agents. I had so much fun just chatting with these two men.

Then as the night was passing, it seemed fairly pleasant, until I turned to see this guy that was threatening toward me. This occurred because I didn't want to marry him. He was the man mentioned earlier who had plans for my inheritance, which were him gaining custody of his daughter with my money. He noticed me and gave me the eyes that he was waiting for me. The fear set in that I was going to lose my life that night. I told these two men (the FBI agents) why this guy was trying to get my attention and the two men told me they would help me. I looked at them and they told me to get in their vehicle and we would make sure this guy would follow us in the woods and sure enough he did. This guy came out with a baseball bat threatening us.

TYING THE THREADS

He began telling me if I didn't go with him, I will pay the price, and that's when these two guys ran after him and tied him up. They messed him up. As I was shaking sitting in this truck but I looked at this guy with strength. I went to see him afterward with these two guys beside me. The two men told him that if he didn't leave me alone this would not end well. He had then told me that he was sorry and that he never meant to hurt me. I looked back and said; *"You already did. You already beat me and you are the one that had me in your arms while you beat me. So do not tell me you never meant to hurt me."* I told him that he was lucky he didn't lose his life and to change his own life. He did.

These series of events lead me to realize I needed a break and I asked a girlfriend if she wanted to come with me to Los Angeles, for a trip. I would cover the expenses and she said yes. I am smiling as I am writing this part because of good memories but a story also. We were to be there for two-weeks. We put on our bathing suites and our snowsuits on top of our luggage bags. That is because in Gatineau, we were in winter days. Quite a weather difference, and our bags were packed and ready. The limousine picked us up and brought us to the Ottawa Airport and we left. This is my pretty woman tale, as you will read.

TYING THE THREADS

We got to Toronto then took the next fast flight to LA. When we got to LA to the Airport it had a little late. We could not find our luggage and we felt stupid because we had only our bathing suites on underneath. We were told to come the next day to the airport, to find our luggage. So, we took a taxi that brought us to this magnificent hotel, for wealthier people. I tried to book the hotel; they didn't know us. One lady had looked at us and told us we didn't belong in this Hotel. I looked at her and said; *"You don't know us, why would you say that."* I looked at my friend and said, *"Okay our money is not good here after all so fine."*

We then went across the street where we were not judged. We ended up having clothes delivered to us from the store until we could go get our luggage, the next day. It had already cost me seven- thousand dollars for the tickets and trip itself. I had brought five-thousand-dollars cash and in those days that was a nice trip.

We visited a few places like the Price is Right on Hollywood Boulevard. Then we mostly hung out on Venice Beach. We were happy with just being there. Cassidy's bar was another place we enjoyed. Our two weeks passed extremely fast but it was the best trip still in my life and even still today.

TYING THE THREADS

On Venice Beach there is a fenced spot which is called Muscle Beach. This was the only time while visiting L.A I saw someone famous. I actually saw Hulk Hogan and the Gladiator Girls. We rollerbladed the whole vacation also, which was really satisfying for us both. We made best memories after such a period of tribulation for myself. It was at this moment that I realized, my teenage years were coming to an end.

PART 2 JUSTIFY

~ Chapter 1 ~
Return from L. A

When I got back from Los Angeles, I of course was living at John's house. I then bought myself a Harley Davidson, a 1340 FLX. It was huge to me but I wanted this specific one. At the time I was very petite. I also had never driven a motorcycle before, but when you're that young nothing really scares you. Some of my friends from Black Lake, Quebec, had come to visit me. They came to visit to teach me how to ride my motorcycle. I practiced on the Highway 50 In Gatineau as the expansion of the highway was built but not yet opened to the public. I did have a lot of falls but came back up and tried again, until I felt ready to go get my motorcycle driver's license.

In our group there were nine men and one woman. John having his three-wheeler was always the first in line, then the older aboriginal man, then me and others in the back. We left Blvd. Lorrain in Gatineau and headed towards Maisonneuve Road, going towards the Interprovincial bridge to go on the Ontario side.

There was a parade that we were going through and before the fast turn to head to the bridge, John turned to us as well as the aboriginal man. then I was looking at the OC Transport Bus coming and since I had to either lean on the right or left…I then stopped at the light. I figured I had time but if I pressed on the gas quickly and I did that.

As I passed I felt the vibration of the bus so close to me, almost missing me and luckily it did miss me. So, I was so proud that I put my feet up on the pegs. I had put my feet up and kept going up the hill. There were people everywhere who were just looking at us and amazed.

They screamed loud *"Wow look at the tiny girl on this motorcycle."* On top of the hill right before the bridge, John was stopped at the red light. I then panicked and forgot to brake since so many people were looking at us all. I then went right into John's back end, hitting him at full speed. The problem is I never let go of the handles and I flew onto the side of the bridge into oncoming cars. The cars were coming and the motorcycle fell on top of me. One handlebar went in my right arm and the peg in my right leg.

TYING THE THREADS

I just remember John standing on top of me and removing my bike slowly and saying that he needed to get my motorcycle to a friend's house close by. I heard a police officer and heard an ambulance. I soon woke up to a doctor telling me It would difficult, if ever I could walk again. After a few months I came out of the hospital in one piece and was working again. I could walk but had scars. I managed to come out of this.

They say if after a fall or an accident you have to get back on your motorcycle or will be afraid forever. I got on my motorcycle that was to be too big for me once again, I thought I was invincible and nothing could stop me. I went to a party in Cala bogie, Ontario with my friends and as we drove there it was fine, but we hardly had any stops to do so it went easy. As we got there, there was a huge hill to actually get to this party and I suddenly felt scared.

A friend Donna Lynn told me to get on her bike she would bring me on top of the hill and she would go back to get my motorcycle and bring it up then I can take over so I can drive myself inside the party. So, after all this I got back on my motorcycle and drove through the party as everyone did and again 1 couldn't stop.

TYING THE THREADS

I drove right into the doors of the barn, so many people saw this, but the thing is; at this party it was full of Outlaws. The party started and I had met someone that we had clicked together and he was an Outlaw himself. After the weekend passed at this party, he asked me if I would go to the Ottawa Exposition with him and I said yes of course.

We parked our motorcycles in a parking lot and we started to walk in and I had my gloves on but soon removed them and held them with me. As we were walking I saw that I had lost a glove and looked at him and had this gut feeling that it was a sign that my motorcycle was gone and I said I wanted to leave. He then asked me why and I said I had this feeling. Sure, enough my motorcycle was not there anymore.

I flipped and ran towards many vans that were around and made them stop for me, so I could look to see if my motorcycle was in their vans. I never found it and I just asked to go home and he brought me home. A week later I had a visit at my home, someone telling me everyone knows this motorcycle is too big for me and to take my insurance money and to buy a smaller motorcycle.

TYING THE THREADS

Others were concerned I could wind up dead or seriously injured. I took it wrong and I felt insulted. A war started because now I knew where my motorcycle was, and then it started. My friend's motorcycle was being targeted and same thing happened until I said no more. I changed my life in some ways, being a motorcycle chick to a California girl dream. I went back to Los Angeles and rented a beautiful Condo al Marina Del Ray. I still had ties to the Tradewinds Hotel, where my friend the owner was. Lived in Los Angeles for month's then came back to Canada for the rest.

When I was in Canada at my house in Alfred, Ontario. I was seeing my girlfriend's brother. His name was Sergio. This was my girlfriend that I had went to Los Angeles with the first time. Me and him had such a sexual passion, it was crazy. We never became boyfriend and girlfriend, because it was better this way. It was a very casual relationship but I also began seeing another man briefly. We kept it this way we couldn't hurt each other, as we were both attractive and not ready. He also had a motorcycle and knew the same people I knew. I would see him each time I would come back from Los Angeles.

TYING THE THREADS

In Los Angeles my friend's name was Devy, he had a sister Cokaty and a brother named Ivan. Me and Devy would go bicycling down at Venice Beach, almost every day. We would do things but Devy believed in not having sex whatsoever until married. Only with the person he really loved. If he didn't love the person he would not. He really loved me and wanted to make me he his queen.

Devy was a billionaire and always had four bodyguards around him at all times. Except when we were alone in the house. For me it was a lonely life, where he would give me money and tell me to get busy. While he was busy doing business. I tried to pass time but loneliness began. At one time we drove to Los Vegas for a weekly trip and again it was like that him with and his four bodyguards. It was me alone and given money to spend on myself. So, living the life there was beautiful, but lonely.

When I got back from Los Vegas, I took the plane to come back, to move out of John's house into a new place in Aylmer, Quebec. I had opened up my own tanning salon here, so I could meet others and make new friends. This new place in Aylmer, had an underground pool and my tanning salon. It was at a corner, merging to the Ottawa River.

TYING THE THREADS

Sergio would meet me at home and we would leave for weeks at a time. I loved him so much. Mutually and it was both our decision to not actually say the words— that we were an item. This way what we felt and experienced was always the best. Three months had passed and I was going back to Los Angeles. I had started to feel a little sick. I took a pregnancy test, before I had even bought my ticket. I found out by this home test that I was pregnant. I didn't believe it so I made a doctor's appointment for the following day. I decided to do this before I headed back to Los Angeles.

I was shocked when I received the telephone call, to tell me that it was true, I was pregnant. I sat for hours, thinking about if I was I ready to have a child. Without hesitations, I said nothing. Nothing to no one in this regard because I wanted this baby for myself. So, my passion with Sergio kept on going and I went to Los Angeles and met with Devy. It was to now tell him. I also had to talk to Sergio back home. I wasn't sure if I still really wanted to tell anyone. I got to my Condo at Marina Del Ray, in Los Angeles and Devy met me there. We ate dinner overlooking all these mansions and boats leaving the harbor.

TYING THE THREADS

We went for a walk, touring around the Marina. There were these ponds on each side of the marina as I recall, and these little red fish would swim by. It was beautiful and peaceful. Devy was one to socially drink but never something strong, like whiskey or anything like that. I forgot to mention that Devy was an Indian man, he was tall and sexy. Because of his religion was why he couldn't have sex, before marriage. He respected that and so did I. I was fine with Sergio, when I was back home. I also know Devy had someone on the side also because I once saw him in the hotel's hot tub with this woman. She had black hair. I had just walked to my bedroom and confronted him the next day. Then I realized I was not in love with him. To me, if he loved me truly, he wouldn't have done this.

I also was not honest back home; I was also doing it so I let it go. So, for me to get even with Devy did not make sense. I went sailing with him back at the Marina, near my condo. I said to him that I had something to tell him. Devy was only wearing a pull-on white shirt; he looked very attractive. I was walking bare foot. When he asked me what I wanted to tell him. I said listen *"I saw you with this girl in the hot tub."*

TYING THE THREADS

I realized that the games have to stop and myself as well, back home. I had an episode and the reality now was that I was pregnant. Well, he went pale and walked towards that bar in the room and filled up a glass with Whiskey and he swallowed it in one second. Devy looked at me and said that I had ruined his dreams. He began crying and I was crying too. The reality is we were hurting each other and I explained to begin wit that I was never happy to always be left alone everywhere.

It frustrated me that he had his bodyguards constantly beside him wherever we went. This was not a life, even though it was paradise in other ways. I told him I loved him but in my heart, but that I couldn't show him anymore. He said to me he had plans to marry me, make love to me and travel the world with me. All this to make me the happiest and richest person on earth.

I believed him and he also told me to think about —if I wanted to keep the baby or have an abortion. I still had time to make a choice. I looked at him and said; *"Devy you have a one-year-old already."* Devy was once married and now divorced. I said although I recognize his religion, I wasn't going to have an abortion.

TYING THE THREADS

This wasn't like me and for me there was a reason I was pregnant. My beliefs were that I was given this pregnancy as a gift of life. We then made the decision of staying friends. I told him to let me know if he ever had a different decision, when my baby was born. For me I could not believe he gave me these two choices. I was so angry that he asked me if I would have an abortion or give my baby away. When he already had a child himself, it felt very conditional. So, I came back home to prepare a plan to hurt him back.

I took the plane and came back from my glamorous life in LA .It was okay because for myself I had inherited money, so I was fine. I knew I would be okay to support my baby, without him. When I got home, I called Sergio and we had a very good evening together. Then the next night, I went to a place in Gatineau, just to see some friends and mingle. Whom do I see? The guy that had threatened me that if I wouldn't marry him, so he could obtain custody of his daughter. He saw me too and smiled. I looked at him with a crooked head because that was too smooth, that he didn't come for me. Then he walked out of the bar and so did a lot of people, and I followed to see what had happened. I could see him walking with an axe in his hands and it looked like he was waiting for someone.

TYING THE THREADS

I thought this was suspicious, a car drove in and I believed this was already planned, I was on edge. Just like when he had attacked me in the past. I watched him make this car stop beside me, where this girl in the car kept screaming to leave her alone. I looked at him and he gazed at me and told me to leave. I refused and he lifted his arms and hit the axe through the windshield of this car. He cut the girl in her neck area, and then he hoped in the car and left with her. I just remember her name and it was Julie or Nathalie. I was traumatized by this and just went home. My head kept racing wondering if what if he came for me again? What did this girl do for him for him to commit such an act? By the time the police came, no one would talk.

I remember that day very well, even if it's a little blurry. I just wanted him to be very afraid of me, with memory of the two big FBI agents. The agents who had brought him to the woods, when I was the one being threatened. I look back and I knew I had my fair share of scaring people in bad ways. Although I had never taken anyone's life. For me my only revenge to lay bare, was my tutor that stole a lot of money from my parents and that had abused me as a child. It turns out, things often go unplanned. I don't know why but God gave me these struggles, but soon I would lose my child.

TYING THE THREADS

This happened because I was doing too much exercising. It took me a while to come back morally. I didn't let Devy know either, because to me he was showing me that it was okay for him to have children already, just not with me.. So, I moved on with my life. To improve myself, I found a job at a gym.

This gym was in Hawkesbury, Ontario. This gym is where I was training, to become Miss Ottawa in fight weights. One month of working in the gym, I met my very best friend Micha. Which we grew closer and we would go out every weekend. After work hours, we would walk the whole main drive in Hawkesbury. We did this for a whole month. On one occasion we saw two limousines drive by and stop beside us. They stopped to ask us if we were interested in going to a Roch Voisine concert, that same night. I couldn't believe it

The back door of the limousine opened, and I saw him. I was such a Roch Voisine fan back then. I sat on stage with Roch. Micha sat with the light guy. I had such an amazing time and I will never forget this concert. Actually, till now that was my only concert I ever went to. After that weekend we started to go out to a bar in Grenville, called the York.

TYING THE THREADS

Our friendship grew and so did our circle of friends, I would say this was my most popular of years. In Los Angeles I had a fancy lifestyle and now a fit lifestyle with many fit friends. Then nearing the end of that summer, Micha got much more comfortable with me. Every time we would go to a bar, she would make me drive her car. Micha was still married but played around. I was single, so I could do what I wanted. My thoughts were to train, train, and train some more. We wanted to win a fit contest and had very little time.

So, my friend Micha left with this guy and she had asked me to drive her car home. She left with this person and her car was not left there of course. I kept it discreet. I had enough of my own in life to deal with. I was still training, and winter was passing. I was almost ready for this competition that was coming month of May.

Spring came; me and Micha were still doing our thing. On weekends we were still going to that same bar, until me and her argued. We argued about the fact that it was unfair that I could never drink, because I was always the designated driver. I could not have fun; we then parted for a week.

TYING THE THREADS

Things of course got resolved, and we of course began to talk again. It was always our same little circle of friends. We were training in my gym that I was working at. We had all decided to adventure a little further and go to another bar, but this time in Mont St-Sauveur, Quebec. Amazing view and place. Micha had a 300 ZX that was so cute and rare for its time. It was a luxury fast car and was exquisite looking.
We headed to this high-class bar, where I guess you could say it was people who had great careers more, than just a gym trainer.

~ Chapter 2 ~

—Part Two —-

He Must Have Been an Angel

We had arrived at this bar and there was a guy that would take your car and park your car for you. It was such a beautiful place to be. So, for me and Micha we started to go there every weekend and each time again I was the one driving the car home. By now she was separated and I was again the designated driver. Alone all the way back home, oh hold on no —not true! I would drive her car to her house sometimes, where I had left my own car. Then I would take my car and go home.

The following weekend, I met a guy. He then asked me what I was doing for work and I had told him I was a flight attendant. Then I got mixed up in my lies and he saw that and I went back again to drive the car home. At this bar you had to dress up fairly fancy. I thought it was fun because I never got to dress up much.

TYING THE THREADS

Mostly better dressed when I used to live in Los Angeles. So, the following weekend came around, but this time it was the entire group of from when we hung around at the York— in Grenville. The group of us decided to go to a bar in Mont St-Sauveur on the following Saturday. Well, I never could have imagined what would happen next. We all walked in together and we were there for about thirty-minutes. We were enjoying the bar and then I glanced over. There was a man sitting at the main bar alone. I thought to myself *"Oh my God for once, here is my style of man."*

He was Tall, with black hair with a goatee. He was well dressed in a black shirt and nice-looking pants. The man had a leather vest that I hadn't seen just yet. I sat beside him and started to talk with him and we were getting along so well. The gentlemen seemed very intelligent and he had my full attention. I turned around to look at my friends and they were all standing there looking shocked, staring at me. They were giving me evil eyes and I turned to continue talking with him. I was wondering as to why they all gave me the evil eyes but I had not addressed it with my friends.

TYING THE THREADS

His name was Peter, as I later found out and his job was a Construction Manager. I saw that he was so very polite and then I looked at his vest and it said "Primitif" HA. I now knew why I had gotten the evil eyes from my friends. So not the same kind of people I was around anymore. My friends were too scared to even come close to me. So, I am the kind of person I will never judge a person by their appearance because I was once there in LA.

My first time arriving to Los Angeles I was judged for what I was wearing. Then judged by my friends, because this was not their kind of people. So, I told Peter my story about my girlfriend Micha, that it had been a whole year I'd be going to bars with her. I couldn't drink because I had to be driving her car. Back and fourth. She would always leave with a different guy each time. I was tired of that because I felt like a puppet with her. I told him I wanted to leave with him. I had already told him names of Richard the Sculpture. I knew my family which was HA and he knew him. So, I knew I was in good hands personally, but they didn't. He wasn't impressed with my friends telling me that if I left with him no one would ever talk to me again. So, I was really sad but determined I wasn't driving this car of hers back home that night.

TYING THE THREADS

For once, I felt an attraction. I had a sexy dress on and felt great. His motorcycle did not have a backseat but I sat behind him and I held on to him for the drive. There were around twenty of us that had went to this bar that night. I did not see the others until we left. As I was leaving, my friends told me I guess it's the last of me because I was going to be taken out that night, I looked at them and said; *"no I wont."*

It was in the back of my head. But I did feel safe with Peter from the beginning. Personally, I would love to see him again, to thank him. We went to his motel room and some other guys started to look in the bedroom and he got up and closed all the curtains He began telling me I was brave. Then he mentioned that if he wasn't big, like he was meaning tall and full of muscles I could have been in serious danger. I asked what kind of danger could I be in? He said woman are not respected in a group, and when someone brings a new girl on site. They intent to go one after the other and have sex with this one girl and that he was protecting me from any of this to happen to me. Peter just wanted to sit with me and we kept talking the whole night.

TYING THE THREADS

Peter said he did this for me so my friend understood she couldn't use me anymore and he said I will bring you home very early, with two of his guys as more protection. He also told me I was lucky that it was him. We never did have sex or anything. This friendship I will never forget and I am thankful for who he was. Peter told me to never do that again because others might not be as friendly and as good a person, such as him. So, I made it home safe, but none of my friends ever talked to me again.

We both lived too far from another and the crest he was wearing what you get when you first get to be in the group. This is your job to be the Primitive. I had respect and will never forget that my life was totally in his hands. He took good care of me and I was very thankful. As a gift I wish I could have sculpted him a Harley to show respect. This story always came with me in my heart Doesn't matter who you are or group you are in— what matters is what's inside a person. Either you're a good person or you're a bad person. It doesn't matter what you do or are, its who YOU are. I have nothing against anyone as long as they are nice to me, RESPECT.

TYING THE THREADS

So, getting back to reality I was heading to be Miss Ottawa, in a few days. With only a few days away from the competition, I had sponsors supporting me. Supporting me throughout this training also. So, everyone from the gym owner, sponsors, and friends were already in Ottawa. They were also there, when I had accident. The accident with my car sitting on the side of the road, out in nowhere land. Back then, there were no cell phones. I sat on the street curb crying while the competition was happening. Me not being there was disappointing and made me feel ashamed. I was screamed at the next day, with so many questions asked.

After I had explained, they understood —but it was my only chance at being Miss Ottawa. I had lost it, and there was only four girls in that specific weight section of the competition. I wanted to beat myself. All the hard work I had put in, the filming of my song with my poses. Plus, the fact of losing all my friends. I quit everything and again made another big change in my life. So, what I did next was leave my job at the gym. I turned the page and moved to Rockland, Ontario. I was looking for a career— a real career. I did not want to have to live a lie anymore. However, before all that, I needed a break and called Sergio and we hung out for a month, while I decided what to do.

TYING THE THREADS

Me and Sergio had the best sex ever. We knew that we couldn't say no to each other. Then after the month had passed by, I still needed some time. I went to Los Angeles for a week. I visited but without seeing Devy. I just needed a real break. Then again found out I was pregnant again. Same way as before, I couldn't believe it. I took a home test, then did a doctor's test that confirmed it all. This time, I was trying to do less exercise— so I wouldn't lose it. I have to believe since it was only between me and Sergio, it was his. Again, I chose not to tell him.

~Chapter 3-Part Two~

Pregnancy Two

Six months into the pregnancy, I was living alone. My neighbors felt sad for me that I was alone and told me they had somebody in mind for me. They had mentioned that he was on his way to their house. They expressed that they wanted me to go over to their place, so I could meet him. This friend was on his way to my neighbour's house; he called me to tell me to get over to his house. Dennis was a married man, married to Susan and they had three children. So, I went over and sat down. I was waiting, and time was passing. Then there was a knock on the door. I became so stressed out, and anxious. Three men came in the house and I had no idea which one was this friend.

I was supposed to meet him, but another one of them noticed me and we couldn't stop looking at each other. My heart was saying *"I hope to God its him."* We clicked instantly and started to talk even before we were formally introduced.

He looked like the hulk to me. He
was tall with black hair and blue eyes.
Full of muscles too, another one just like
Peter from Mont St-Sauveur, only not a
biker. I was happy but then told myself
"No Louise, not him." That that was
Juliano and I just said I apologize, I do
not feel so good. I also said I had to see
if he would find me again. I saw them
leave and that was it for a bit. Till the
next week afterward. He came and
knocked on my door alone this time.

I answered the door and was wowed
again and let him inside of course. We
kissed and talked. He told me about his
situation and how he felt so lost. He
explained to me that in between all this,
there was a bet to who was going to have
me. He didn't think that it was funny. We
had really clicked and fell in love that
day. Reality was that he was married and
had two daughters. I felt so sad and he
said that he was staying with me and
never going back. He called his wife right
in front of me to tell her. I think I was in
shock at the same time. I felt so bad for
her. I had never been in that situation
before but I just saw happiness.

Roberto was the love of my life and
we hit it off so fast. He never had sex
with me until the day he moved in.
Which was four-days after we met. I
wasn't sure what was happening but I
wasn't refusing this feeling either.

TYING THE THREADS

All I remember was by then I was six-months pregnant. I had never told the father I was pregnant either, because I wanted this child alone. Me and Roberto started our journey and we lived together very happily. We had to go through a lot of things together, because he had hurt another woman to be with me. His divorce cost him a lot of money, but it was his choice. Roberto's parents were just like mine. I was not shown that they had a lot of money growing up too. Mind you they had a huge home of seven-thousand square feet, plus a huge double garage, unattached from the house. They also had 150 acres included with the home, we grew up in. Other people knew they were rich but not me.

Robertos parents were adorable and they accepted me in the long run, but it took a while. Just like my parents, we always had Christmas parties at his parent's house. By that time, I had my son and Roberto had his daughters. Two beautiful daughters, which one of them lived with us. Two more years had passed and his father was sent to the hospital with a broken arm. This is when they found out that it was because cancer was eating his bones in his arm. This had been going on for a while. His father was the mason that built the Campeau's House, in Toronto. You know all these rocks that were put on this Kumongous house.

TYING THE THREADS

The house was a seven-thousand square feet. Robertos father soon passed away and then for his mother it was very difficult. Just like my mother had missed her husband a lot in that matter also. One year later she also passed away. I believe that if you are in a relationship for over thirty-years and one passes away, it's very hard. You just miss the other one so much. When aging, you need each other more and the fact that you are all of sudden alone is hard. When you are sure the other one is not coming back because they have passed away—you collapse with pain.

I still believe even to this day, that God wanted me to have a good life. I know God wanted to give me someone that truly loved me and give me a family. Roberto had three brothers and they were all married. So, when the disbursements would come, he had questions of whom would get the house. Who would be buying it and give shares to the brothers or sell the house. We had offered to buy it, and afterward to separate the money that was in the bank. Which would have given us each one-hundred- thousand dollars. We bought the house and put thirty- thousand dollars down on the house. Our new mortgage of one-hundred and fifty, thousand dollars. The house was seven- thousand square feet and had 150 acres.

TYING THE THREADS

It was so beautiful, then we soon got married on a huge boat with guests on the Ottawa River. Our lives were starting to get a lot better. When Roberto married me, he adopted my son also. When we first moved into the home, we fixed the driveway ourselves, all in cement. Then we got some wood to build a horse fence, taking up around fifteen acres of land. We rented our property to a farmer for corn. Roberto built a huge playset for the kids to play on and we bought a truck.

A beautiful year had passed. We spent our time working on the farm and building things. We felt so happy, my life was so beautiful and my sister was also back in my life. My sister now saw me as stable and loved Roberto also. We had a horse and a dog named Keisha. Our families were united and I could not have asked for better family.

Now was really the time for me to get a career. Since time had passed and I never had the previous time to do this and I choose to be a Medical Laboratory Assistant. So, I went to Career Canada College. It was a 6-month condensed course. We even did a water course; it was a little river in our back yard. We had built a bridge, so that our son could go fishing right in our own backyard.

TYING THE THREADS

Then I broke a huge mirror and it was also a prelude of things to come. We then got new neighbors that would change our lives forever.

~Chapter 4~

Neighborhood Changes

D o you Recall a movie called "*The Good Son?*" We seen our new neighbors move in next door and we noticed they had children. Two of them were around my son's age. They were on our street, on our side of the road too. We were three distant houses away from them. On the other side of the road there were also three houses, but they were not newer builds. They had moved right across from us. There were many children in the neighbourhood around our sons age and many he had already befriended. My son was always playing with the neighbourhood kids for a year at least before these new neighbours moved in front of us. Like anyone we welcomed them and their kids. Just their youngest son would come play at our house. Their youngest daughter was not very playful, mostly stayed home.

I never questioned anything. They all seemed like good people, but a little rough to the looks. Like earlier in my story— I told you, I don't judge anyone. Horror movies had always been on television, and a least probable outcome for my reality.

TYING THE THREADS

I might have seen something or two during my life but what I am about to tell you was at my house, where we had built our future. Where we had our first chance to make it in life. A chance at peace and love. We were so young still, and we were close to retirement. Also because of the work we put in, we didn't owe so much to the bank anymore. Roberto was a Superintendent for a Construction company. He was making very good money and sometimes he took jobs on the side. We were almost done paying everything.

I would show up at school with hay on my nursing uniform, from cleaning the horse stalls in the morning before leaving for school. Then when we would be home, and their son would show up in his jeans and shirt. The neighbours son always had a chain to his wallet just like what an adult would wear. It really was the appearance of a bully, if you looked at him. However, he was very polite this boy. To the looks he looked intimidating and I was about to find out pretty quickly just how much.

Later to find out he didn't just look like it, but they had a big past into it. Even for me to write it, it makes me shake because I never like having to tell this story again.

TYING THE THREADS

I should say that in the same year in 1998. In Quebec we had the ice storm that gave us a lot of work on the farm. They had moved in next door to us on the first of August 1998, one month before school was to resume. The first week or so, we would only see them once a week coming to play. In the second week, they would always comment that we were rich. I kept saying that we worked hard to buy this and to get where we are. We were laughed at by all of them— including the kids.

Then after learning a bit more about them, the father had teenage girls and the woman that lived with him was his new girlfriend. They met in Vanier, Ontario and this was their chance also and to be together starting a new life. Then the weekend would come to pass.

The mother and father had left to go do some groceries and only the oldest of the teenage girls was home. My son and him which I'll name him Hugo were playing together alone around our houses. At some point I saw my son run home crying and I asked him what's wrong and he told me that Hugo and his half-sister had put him in the dryer and they had started it for a minute or so with him in it. I was shaken by this and by the time I started walking to their home, their mother had just arrived back home.

TYING THE THREADS

I remember I had a cup of coffee in my hands when I walked next door. As I got to her door she greeted me nicely and said; *"Would you like to come in."* I explained why I was there and what had happened. The half sister and Hugo were looking at me with the evil eyes. To me I just explained to the mother what had happened and the mother turned around with her fist and threw a big punch in her son's stomach. This punch was a very hard hit and I said; *"I'm sorry to have came over to disclose this."* There was no need to punch him and she told me this was the way she dealt with her children. I just walked home shaking like a leaf and feeling so bad for the son.

I felt really awful still and we are now into the next day— which was a Saturday. The son came over to play with our son, he was invited to have dinner with us. They played hide and seek inside the house. They also went fishing in the backyard with the two other little neighbors. I was in the house doing some cleaning, cooking, and watching from the kitchen window. The kitchen window gave me a clear view of the backyard, but my eyes were not always looking in the backyard, as I was doing a few things.

TYING THE THREADS

Then all of a sudden, I hear my son coming in the house and he was crying hard and loudly. My son only ten years old. I asked him what was wrong? My son then told me that while they were fishing, Hugo had thrown his sunglasses under the bridge and threatened my son that if he didn't go get his sunglasses, he would push him off the bridge. So, my son had then gone to pick them up, but he was afraid by this type of behavior from his friend. For us, we were in shock because we had never seen anyone be so demanding or behave this way.

Was he being playful or was this who he really was? To me it was children being children and having a bad day. Also, I was afraid myself to go tell their mother about this one episode. I was fearful she would hurt her son even worse. I knew I had to tell her anyways. I then called her and hung up after she said she would deal with it. Then I had said they would take a week's break saying everyone in their own yard, for a few days. This way it was kind of a punishment, so that nothing like this would ever happen again.

Everyone was in their own yard, and Monday had passed, Tuesday passed, and then Wednesday— Hugo showed up. Hugo then came over asking if they could play. My son said; *"Please mom."*

TYING THE THREADS

I figured two-days would have been a good break. The day went by without anything happening. However, that day I had learned a little about them. The oldest son had taken out a picture from a frame. In this picture was an adult toy. I was in shock and just so stunned I couldn't even move an inch. I asked why he took this picture out. I just remember his answer being that this was a way his mother was punishing him. Then he had told me that her mother's brother was a bad man but I just couldn't handle listening to that. I wondered if it was all a joke to pull my leg. Even though I was shaking, I had so much to do at home, that I had forgotten our conversation.

One day my sister-in-law showed up and I hadn't seen her in so long. I sat with her and we were talking and then I received a telephone call from Hugo. Hugo was not asking me but telling me to go pick him up. He was at this little store in St-Pascal. This store was about a mile down the road from my house. I answered politely, but weary. I began questioning him as to how did he get to the store? Hugo told me he was ridden on the back of his half-sisters bicycle. I asked him if she was there to bring him back.

TYING THE THREADS

Hugo then began screaming at me
*"Yes she is but you are going to come get
me or else*! I was in shock and even my
sister-in-law could hear this discussion
and said politely that I had company
and that I couldn't go get him. My sister
told him to come back with his sister and
he hung up the phone, while chanting
mean words. I didn't quite hear them. I
was rather distraught from this telephone
call.
        Even the lady at the store
remembered him because he had to ask
her to use the telephone behind the cash
register. When my sister-in-law left,
Hugo was at the end of my driveway and
gave me this look. A look like an adult
would make out of anger. I just went
back in the house and thought nothing of
it and Roberto had to work late in that
day, I would say 9PM.

        I then received a telephone call
from the oldest brother. The eldest
brother started telling me that it was his
mother that made him call. He was
calling to see if I could pass her some
cigarettes. I answered with the truth,
which was that I only had three cigarettes
left. I wasn't able to give any, and he
answered me by laughing. He then said;
*"You guys are rich and you don't have
any cigarettes?"*

~ Chapter 5 ~

Flames of Evil

The mother took the telephone from her son and was saying the same thing while laughing. I began trying to explain that what we had, we worked for. I explained that we owed some to the bank and that we weren't rich. I did hope that one day soon we wouldn't have to work anymore. Then it was over when Roberto came home.

The next day the weekend had begun; it was a Friday. The son had come over "Hugo" and had asked me if he could come for dinner. Of course, I said yes that he was welcome to stay over for dinner. Then he came down in the basement with all of us and watched the movie Water World. Hugo asked questions during the movie in regard to the content. This was Hugo's way to lean in on our home. Me and Roberto went to bed, not too long after. They kept watching movies— So we thought.

Hugo had told Michel to follow him into the shed. This was so he could prepare a mixture of oil and Gas. Which was shown in the movie.

TYING THE THREADS

Michel was always under a threat but we had no idea just how bad in this moment. How can you know a young child would know how crimes work? Me and Roberto would always wake up around 530AM to go feed the horses and start our day. We were locked in our bedrooms from the outside, so were the other doors. We both panicked and wondered how that happened and who did this. After managing to get out and figuring who did this. Hugo said that it was a joke.

My son Michel looked pale. They both went to play in their pyjamas in the basement, until breakfast was ready. When they both sat at the table, Michel looked even more pale. Hugo looked kind of excited. Which then I noticed that I could smell gas. At first I thought maybe it was a gas leak, that had happened inside the house. Even to be writing this today is still so hard on me. I took many breaks to be able to finish writing this part.

Then suddenly, they just looked at each other and Hugo spoke up right away explaining that they were playing hide and seek, where the oil tank was in the basement. Hugo proclaimed that they probably had some on their clothes and not to worry. We then ate our breakfast and they went to play outside. I began the dishes and started to clean the house.

TYING THE THREADS

At some point Michel and his father had built a tree house on our property. This treehouse was maybe a mile down our property, it was build prior, before they had moved in. I went and looked in the front window and saw that the other neighbours were outside. They were named Meli and Hank. Meli and Hank were also headed alongside Michel and Hugo, toward the tree house. I did not see a brick or should I say I didn't even think there was a threat, because you don't think someone so young is capable of this. So, I continued with my cleaning and it didn't take very long before I heard screams. I went to look and I saw Meli and Hank run towards their house quickly, they were crying and screaming frantically.

I saw Hugo coming straight toward me and he said; *"Michel is on fire and he is stuck to a tree."* Hugo ran home. As I turned to start running in the woods to get my son, he was already a few feet away from me. I stopped and saw the cloud's of smoke moving around him, without realizing he was on fire.

I saw the flames coming out of his whole body and then it hit me, I realized he was on fire. I opened my arm and he then collapsed in my arms softly. He kept on asking me *"mama I won't die right."* My son kept saying this over and over.

TYING THE THREADS

I told one neighbour to call the ambulance right away. Meli and Hank's mother came over and we put a wet blanket around my son and it was taking a long time for the ambulance to get to us or at least it felt that way.

The worst part is that my husband had already left for work and I didn't know how to reach him. All this happened on the 27th of August in 1998. A few days before school started. Finally, the firefighters got to our house. One of the firefighters did not know what to do, since my son's face was all burned. If he should put the mask on his face or not. We both looked at each other while he put the mask over my sons face so he could breathe but it melted into his face. We couldn't remove it now.

Then all of a sudden, the ambulance got there also and PA. One of the paramedics was telling me they were sorry that they were late. *"So sorry"* he said to us. I thought okay but now its time to go PA. I had known PA, since I was a child myself. He was so stressed out when he saw that it was my son. He picked me up by the back of my pants and lifted me into the ambulance. The police were in front of us. One was in the back of the ambulance the whole way to the Hospital.

TYING THE THREADS

It was just like in a movie where my son entered a empty white room with all the accessories of the Hospital room. I saw them put everything on my son, while all the doctors were rushing around in this room. The doors were closed and I couldn't even be in there. Then came the waiting.

So, while I am waiting for any updates about my son. Soon there was a lady from Social Services preparing me, in case the worst would happen. There was another lady around, who was just sitting on the other side of me crying. She was looking at me and saying: *"I really hope your son does pull through."* I kept on looking at this other lady and I felt something bizarre. You know that weird feeling inside of you—intuition.

My husband then arrived at the Hospital and I immediately ran to him and collapsed into his arms. I began explaining what had happened and that I knew nothing yet. We sat for hours, but we he had to go back home for the horses. I just didn't want to leave the Hospital.

~ Chapter 6 ~

A Mothers Tears of Agony

"I am crying while typing this out, it is still very hard for me to relive these moments."

Many hours later, doctors started to come out of the room. One came towards me, while the lady from Social Services and this other lady were there wanting to listen to this conversation. The doctor told me that my son is in a coma and seems to be doing fine. However, it would take days before we could really know if he would come out of all this okay. I exhaled and collapsed. Then this other lady was holding me.

I held her back and she kept on following me. I was really clueless to who she was. They had brought my son into the intensive care unit. As I am walking towards the doors of the intensive care unit, all news crews were there— waiting for a story. I had security helping me to get into the ICU. I was not aloud to speak to anyone. For days I sat beside my son's bed.

TYING THE THREADS

I was looking at him with all the tubes, and oxygen machines. My sons ears had melted, and his eyes almost separated in two. I kept looking at all the burns he had. I kept crying and asking God why us, thinking how could this happen. All these questions ran through my head while crying and waiting for my son to come back coherently. The other lady that was there, I later found out who she was. She was waiting for my son to pass so she could have his organs for her daughter.

Then maybe a few days later I lifted my head and it was like I had seen an angel. It was my cousin Daniella telling me it would be okay and that he will come out strong. I cried and she said I am here. I almost collapsed, then a nurse came in and told me to go home and to get some sleep. It was on the 5th day and I hadn't showered or anything yet. Still waiting and exhausted.

I decided that I would take a one-night break. As I got home and entered my home, many people were inside and many flowers were brought to us. Gina and her two kids came over to support us. Meli and Hank started to tell us that Hugo had went around the street saying to all other neighbours that he was going to put gasoline all around our house.

Hugo also said he would take his
father's firearm and fire from the street
and blow up our home. I started shaking
like crazy. I soon called the police.
Which
they then took the son Hugo and the
mother to the Rockland Police Station.
It took Hugo hours to admit but he did at
some point. The mother asked
him why. I didn't wait for the answer, I
ran back to the Hospital —as I
really didn't know any answers to
anything yet. I was just so afraid. With
the treats and all that had already
happened police were only able to charge
the father for not keeping his shotgun
locked up.

Do not forget this information as it
will become important later on in my
story. This mother and her son had talked
to the Ottawa Paper while we were in the
Hospital. The mother had said that her
son was the hero for saving my son's life
to the writer for the Ottawa Paper.

I couldn't believe my eyes and
ears— as I had promised him the story
when I could. I still have a picture of that
clip at home now to look at and wonder
about. It was the farthest truth from what
really happened to my family. I made the
choice that my concentration needed to
be at the Hospital and to make sure my
son came out alive.

TYING THE THREADS

Then a few days later we had investigators sit us down in our home, in our basement. Investigators explained to us how it all happened, with their investigation. My son and others were brought by force into the woods, where a brick would be used if my son and others didn't walk ahead to arrive to the tree house. They would be hit by that brick. Hugo then had Meli and Hank tie my son to a tree, while under threat.

Hugo had a bottle of gas mixed with oil and created a spark to ignite it. Which he then sprayed it all on my son's face and body. Hugo then watched him burn. Meli and Hank had time to run away, which is the reason why Hugo was right behind trying to get them both. My son Michel had managed to set himself free from the rope and ran home. This is why he wasn't moving before he collapsed into my arms. While we were in the house trying to save my son, the mother of Hugo and Hugo had thrown his clothes for evidence inside the back garbage. The two then tried to get involved with information.

The investigators looked at me and my husband said to us *"Well you can go next door and kill them, but who will the at the Hospital with your son?"*

TYING THE THREADS

Me and my husband looked at each other and cried. I said to Roberto; *"I need you, please don't do anything. God will take care of it. "*

Hugo was two weeks shy of being twelve years old, he could not be charged. The next day I called children's services to be told that they talked to the mother of Hugo and that she was the guardian of Hugo. As long as she could provide, children's services said that she could still provide care for him. Despite Hugo almost taking my sons life.

Apparently he was fine to stay home— without even a slap on his fingers. I called the police and asked is there anything anyone will do? The police said because of Hugos age nothing could be done. We were all scared for our lives. Michel of course we were afraid to bring him back home from the Hospital.

The next day I received a call from Hugo's mother, trying to say she was sorry and so was Hugo. The mother then asked if she could bring Hugo to the Hospital to visit Michel. I panicked and said of course not. She said she wanted to show Hugo what he had done. I responded that I didn't want him to be near us again— whatsoever.

TYING THE THREADS

I then hung up the phone, never understanding the way these people were thinking. It was mind-blowing to me— the audacity. They never failed to amaze me. Now indulging in a second attempt to go home, I had to shower and relax, I left the Hospital and soon heard a knock on the door. It was this mother and Hugo showed up at my door with a suitcase.

The mother began asking me if Hugo could stay at my house, until my son was to come back home from the Hospital. My head turned sideways, as I was looking at them. They however looked clueless. Everyone in my house was in shock listening to this woman. I said; *"Are you serious?"*… How in the name of God or where do you see that I would have time to keep your son, while my son is in the Hospital fighting for life?" They said to me; *"Well, you have seven bedrooms and the house must feel empty!"* I turned around and said; *"Please don't come back to my house."*

The nerve of these people I thought to myself, I couldn't believe the audacity of these people. It was like they had no brains. Or so I thought, because in the end you will see.

~ **Chapter 7** ~

Goodbye Horses

I was so angry that our Justice System was not protecting us whatsoever. It was just unbelievable, just like nothing had happened at all. Then my son was slowly waking up and the only pictures of him that existed were when he got to the Hospital, which were taken by the Investigators. It was like they didn't want anyone to see the truth. We were forbidden to take pictures, no one was aloud other than them. It took six-months, before my son came out from the coma.

Most are aware that going to the Hospital daily is expensive. The costs of parking, eating, and gas. I had obviously quit my course, with the promise that I could continue when things would be better for my family. So, my husband had to be the provider. My husband had to continue to work, to be able for us to keep our trucks on the road, and our home financially stable. I couldn't help and that was difficult for me.

TYING THE THREADS

Once my son was home I never let him out of the house. I was later approached by Rony from the Local newspaper company. He had asked us if we needed donations. I had said no because I had no clue how costly this was going to be. I thought we would be okay.

We had what we had. I didn't want another person to call us rich. I did not want to take money when we had some money. I didn't want to be perceived as Hugo and his family had seen us. We ended up purchasing a whole hamster cage with miles of tubing. We did this so Michel could play in the house and not be too bored. I lived in fear; I never let anyone come play with him.

Later on, I would a receive a call from the mother of Hugo, telling me that they were sorry and that they were going to move. I explained that they didn't have to move. I also explained that we will we have to be close to the Hospital, and that our family lawyers had advised us of this. This started something new, some more victimization for us. While I was taking care of our son, I had started to write a Bill C-3 that I wanted to present to the Minister of Justice, in Ottawa Ontario.

TYING THE THREADS

I wanted them to implement this, because of my own families tragedies. Money at home was running tight. I had begun to make appointments to meet lawyers. One by one we screened for a lawyer. We had met with my husband's family lawyers as well, which were also notaries. Today I look back and now know how important it is to make sure that when you hire a lawyer —to make sure they possess expertise in the field they work in.

Our family Lawyers who were the Notaries, are the ones that approached us and told us they would take the case. They advised that we should move closer to the Hospital. They told us to sell everything for peanuts, but not to worry about a thing they would get us our money back. You have to remember that the rest of my inheritance and Roberto's— were all put into our family home.

Us having worked hard, to try to pay for the rest of what we owed. Back then $375,000 was a lot of money. We were left with owing maybe around $65,000 when we sold our home for $145,000. I trusted these lawyers —sadly. So, while we left it all in the lawyers' hands, we had three more months at this house to prepare to sell a few things. The things we sold included our horses.

TYING THE THREADS

Most things we had from inside the house were also sold. Remember this was a 7000 square foot home. It was very painful to sell our horses I will never forget the tears I cried. While the lawyers were preparing our case, I was meeting with each one of the Ministers of Justice. One by one, I began to share my story. Some were in agreement with me. Some were curious about what this child's background was and felt sorry that it happened. There must be a story behind it some expressed. It changed absolutely nothing in the end. It took me one year of my life to meet them all. It only made me feel even more unheard and frustrated.

My lawyers told us they were asking millions on this case and not to worry about a thing. They were asking for money for our house, and pain and suffering. It was expressed that we would receive millions for Michel to care for him. This was in case he couldn't get a career, it had caught the eyes of the owner of the Insurance Company, our case specifically. Our life was changing so quickly. Inside of yourself, it feels like you are scared but at the same time you don't show it to others. I had to remain strong. I had to act like nothing could bring me down.

TYING THE THREADS

A young couple had bought our house and we had rented a place in Orleans, Ontario. We had a six- month contract and we gave them $18,000 to cover the rent. We explained why we needed to be there and we paid cash for this rental.

~ Chapter 8~

Bad Company

We put our trust and our lives in these lawyers' hands. I kept taking care of my son until it was moving day to Orleans. Then I sat beside my son's bed, because the sound of his breathing was keeping me awake. He was breathing so loud and I knew it wasn't right. Again, my mind was running rampant as to why he was breathing this way. I made a doctor's appointment and he told me that he tried to get access to see his file and from the hospital. The file was going up and down and it was impossible to view it. The doctor also knew something wasn't right.

Time was just passing by. No one was able to tell me what and why my sons breathing was so hard. No one was able to answer me so I remembered that the Shriner's had given me a plane ticket to go and it included a return trip, if I ever needed it to go to Boston to the Shriner's Hospital. So, I told Roberto my plan and we left the next day— the three of us by plane.

TYING THE THREADS

When we got there, they took Michel in right away and did some tests. Doctors came back out; they were dressed in their attire with masks. They told us it was an emergency and that Michel needed to be operated within the next five-days or he would be gasping for air, since he had breathed in flames of fire. The fire had burned his vocal cords and they needed to re-open his trachea. Then they told us it was our decision on what to do. I looked at my husband and the Doctors and said it is; *Isn't there's Doctors that do this in Ottawa?* and they explained yes but there is no time. I mentioned to my husband in front of them we have the men coming to pick up the horses.

I wanted to say goodbye to the horses and I wanted to make sure that they were going to a good home. I was reassured they weren't going to be used for food. I looked at the Doctors and explained that I would find a doctor in Ottawa, that would do the procedure. I explained that they were talking about us staying in Boston for at least five-months. They looked at me and said; *"Well it's up to you, but if we go back home there is a chance Michel might not make it."* This was because he was struggling badly to breathe.

I thank God, that I had found the ticket from the Shriners. I also thanked the Doctors for confirming what I thought was happening. A mothers intuition. We then took the plane back home to find a Doctor in Ottawa. The airline company had me sign a paper for them, basically ensuring that if Michel died on the plane on our way home—-it would be on my shoulders.

I looked at them very angry and said that wasn't fair to say this. It was not a very nice thing to be told. I told them we came by plane, and we are leaving by plane. I was so scared inside myself, but we got back to Ottawa safely.

I had a days to find a Doctor in Ottawa. I had to think quickly, and I did find one. A very nice Doctor who specialized in her field, she was very kind, and smart. She asked me for his file and I made sure she had the file, plus the information given by the Boston Doctors.

My son's birthday is on January 3rd, 1988. By the third day, I had found a doctor. Miss Kay was her name and she was scheduled to do this operation a month from the day.

TYING THE THREADS

In the meantime, I had time to go visit the Papanack Zoo and try to get pictures of my son with the white Lions. These lions were rare, so rare that Michael Jackson had even came down to try to purchase one of them. Of course, without success.

My son took pictures with one of the lions in his arms. I had the picture arranged so you could see the lions in the picture. I had one signed by Celine Dion and the other by the Rougeau Brothers. I arranged a press Conference to be passed to local News, just so I could carry this out as my plan. My plan was to show the doctor in the news that was going to do the operation. I was trying to sell these photos to be able to get funds. The funds were to be divided between the Hospital Zoo, The Shriners Hospital, and our family.

It worked because the doctor listened to me and never cut my son's throat. They put a temporary bone there. She knew if she would have made a mistake it would likely end up in the news. I also had letters from Hospital and the Shriners supporting my son. A countdown was coming for our first mediation. A mediation between us, our lawyers, and the insurance lawyers. The defendants were also there. The discussions started and I felt so edgy.

TYING THE THREADS

I had to face them. Our lawyers started to explain to them what was asked. Then the President of the insurance company walked in and said I can't wait to see what the outcome will be. I looked and just listened. Then it didn't take all of a few minutes before the insurance lawyer started to laugh, how inappropriate given the circumstances. The unthinkable would be said...

They looked at my lawyers and told us all that there is a clause that says that any criminal outcome is not insurable for a claim. He also told us, that it seemed that it was my own lawyers mistake and that it was to up to my lawyers to pay us for their mistake. As this claim was not insured.

Well let me tell you how upset I was, because from the beginning I trusted my lawyers. I just walked out with because everyone just laughing. I felt so lost and angry. It seemed there was no justice or help for my family and we then left and went home. Another reminder of how life is always trying and never free from more devastation. Things were supposed to change for the better. The injustices kept coming and again my character would be tested and no relief would come. The help and relief we counted on and needed would simply just not exist. The anger and frustration I felt was decimating.

~Chapter 9~

The Move

Now its moving week to our house to Orleans. Moving well the rest of our things, what was left after everything was said and done. There was no going back— it was sold. After the mediation, we came back home to finish packing and organizing things. We began driving down our street and we see them standing there smiling. Well, I finally lost it and started running after them with a baseball bat and my husband stopped me. I was screaming "WHY? WHY? WHY? So, we went inside our home and started relaxing. I felt like I was about to turn into a monster. I wasn't a monster and this wasn't really me. The evening carried on and we went to bed after a much defeating day.

Around midnight I hear my fax machine going off, this got me up to go look of course. It was a letter from our lawyers wanting me to sign them off the case and to let them go. I was livid and I was angry to even have to deal with these lawyers. I never signed the paperwork.

TYING THE THREADS

I then called them the next day to let them know that I will fight this and this wasn't right. Not only did this happen to our son, and to us, but now with our own lawyers. Nothing made sense to me anymore. I felt like it was an opportunity to make us lose everything —including ourselves. I started to write the Law Society. I explained what had happened but it was a wait for answers. In the meantime, I tried to retain another lawyer and my husband would drive me to do it. So, this first lawyer I had encountered was a criminal lawyer. I sat and waited for him to come out of his office. I anxiously explained my story to him, soon after.

He looked at me and said to me in his exact words. *"You know I could put you in jail for everything you're telling me. because I represent the criminal typically, and not a person like you."* I ran out while crying and running to my husbands car, where he was parked. I just turned and looked at to say; *"let's go home."*

Now the only thing I could think about was to have get even with my previous lawyer. I felt angry and full of revenge. This was so out of character for me, I would never hurt a fly. I was starting to become a mean person and on a revenge mission.

TYING THE THREADS

As a mother experiencing this type of trauma and feeling. So betrayed and defeated, I became full of anger. I always talked myself down and gained my clarity again. I often wondered what would make me finally lose it. What would be the final straw? I always remained a good person in spite of it all. Here I am but thirty-years later, writing this book. I still experience pain caused from other people without understanding most of the whys. I often wonder what I did to deserve this reality. It felt like I was being punished in many ways.

I received a letter from the Law Society, getting my lawyers to Register themselves, that they were responsible for making a huge mistake. I really felt like this was the last thing my family had needed, to be in conflict with the people who were supposed to help and protect us. I felt that I had already been through enough with our son's accident alone. I had lost my inheritance and Roberto's inheritance, and everything we had worked for. I had refused to ask for donations and when I asked a year later, I was told by the man at the local newspaper company no. He refused and said that I should have said yes when the accident happened.

TYING THE THREADS

Basically, he felt people would want new stories and mine was old now. It felt as if the media help was conditional on views and interest. This was disappointing to me. As a result of having to move, we had already lost $1.5 million between selling everything quickly and for under market value. We incurred major losses, while our lawyers assured us that they would recover the money during litigation. The almost the death of our son, these people never even received a slap on their hands, not even a dent. So now I felt like Erin Brockovich, trying to figure it all out.

Soon after another The Law Office contacted me to say they would help us. At this point we are now at my son's third operation to re-open his throat, and countless visits to the hospital to treat his burns. Burns that covered his entire body and required extensive care.

The new Lawyers took our case on the 25th of July in 1999. In those days the statue of limitations was five years to sue your lawyers or you would lose your case. Well, they put us to sleep, telling us that they would try getting the insurance back in to negotiate, but never talking about things with the first lawyers. The first lawyers who took the case to begin with. I explained my case.

TYING THE THREADS

Well, we always received settlement letters, that they sent to the insurance for five-years to the day, it was coming close to that five- year closure. I looked at them and said you guys are something else. It felt like there was a dark cloud trying to make me lose my mind even further. I felt rage and violence but that little angel on my shoulder always kept me safe. Reminding myself that I wasn't myself and I wasn't crazy. but what will make me lose it one day. I often wondered *"Why do I remain a good person if everyone is just testing my family?* I will say it took my son taking his two hands and placing them on me saying; *"Mom we lost everything I understand its not fair but be strong mommy."* I had to be strong for my son, deep inside I felt that.

I was trying to understand so much around me, mostly what the heck was wrong with my life. Even my own mind, didn't feel like home anymore. Today still I can say that even if I try to figure out what went wrong, I cant seem to understand it. I often wondered if my brain moved too quickly, and aimlessly. Other parts of my mind perhaps. Numb.

I felt we had been victimized multiple times, and it was becoming a pattern. A pattern of profound and life changing events.

TYING THE THREADS

Life would continue on and still I would often wonder why things seemed so tough. I would begin looking for steady work to help get things back under control. I stumbled upon a job position at a known Money Transporting Company.

It is one of the most known money transporting in the world. It meant I had to do all positions. Transporting, guarding, and driving around with the cash. I would have to become proficient in all these skills, before I could get on the top list of Drivers. I had to do money room, guarding, and messenger tasks. It was such a cool job because I had to learn how to use firearms and understand the laws about them.

I worked there for four-years and by then of course we lived in Navan, Ontario. Since we had moved a few times, I had told my husband to get a trailer. I told him to put all his tools that we took out of our seven- thousand square foot house from the garage in there. So, I am sure you can imagine we had a lot. The same day we moved the tools into our trailer, it all was robbed. We tried to call the Insurance Company the next day. We wanted to see if we could receive any help with this. We received an answer later on that day.

TYING THE THREADS

They told us that because they were his working tools for his company, they needed a different insurance type of insurance coverage for a claim to be made. We didn't have that type of coverage. Again, we experienced more loss, we had just lost over $75,000 worth of tools. A continuation to the pattern of loss. I was beginning to become increasingly more frustrated and left feeling hopeless. I was only thinking what I could do to teach someone a lesson. I was full of the need for revenge, but again I had my little angel inside talking to me. My angel would say; *"Louise, please stay a good person. You are Loved"*.

Although things were continually challenging, I still had my little angel telling me that it was not who I was and one day everything would make sense. I would see there other people who were awful and that nothing would happen to them. Sometimes thing happen in our lives that are beyond our control. Despite life's seasons of pain, tragedy, and waves of despair, it is important that we remain loyal to ourselves and continue on the path of growth.

Let the threads represent the struggles of life. We are either bound by the threads or create new patterns. Life can be full of unjust, unfair, and full of life altering moments.

TYING THE THREADS

During my own struggles and successes, I had to remain humble, strong and full of love for my family. It was the love for my family and for my son that kept me hanging on. I learned resilience during the most painful moments s a family had to endure.

Sometimes life wont be easy, its always a bit heavy but never lose yourself or the love you have for others. Never get lost in the pain and sufferings other may cause, because its about them and not YOU. The betrayals that you face, let God handle them, because he saw it all.

I share my story of my younger years, but the story doesn't end there. The battles will always come but what comes next, no one could predict.

~ ABOUT THE AUTHOR ~

LOUISE BARRETTE

Louise Barrette is from Canada. Louise grew up in the rural areas of Alfred, Ontario. Louise is a woman of many talents, including sculpting. She enjoys music, writing and spending time with her loved ones. Louise is a down-to-earth individual, with an unmatched level of resilience.

Her big heart and kind soul will always be her guiding light on her life journey. Louise has a background in fitness, Health and Safety Officer in

TYING THE THREADS

Civil, nuclear construction and security.
Louise loves the beach and horses.
Growing up in rural areas, she
appreciates nature and the simple things.
Louise is dedicated to advocating for her
family and the people she loves. Her
drive to keep moving forward has always
fueled her success and this series of
books.

TYING THE THREADS

TYING THE THREADS

TYING THE THREADS